BECAUSE OF MIGUEL

AuthorHouse™
1663 Liberty Drive
Bloomington, IN 47403
www.authorhouse.com
Phone: 833-262-8899

Because of the dynamic nature of the Internet, any web addresses or links contained in this book may have changed since publication and may no longer be valid. The views expressed in this work are solely those of the author and do not necessarily reflect the views of the publisher, and the publisher hereby disclaims any responsibility for them.

This book is printed on acid-free paper.

ISBN: 978-1-6655-7969-8 (sc)
ISBN: 978-1-6655-7970-4 (e)

Library of Congress Control Number: 2023900315

Print information available on the last page.

Published by AuthorHouse   01/27/2023

authorHOUSE®

For all those who teach and love reading

2

Because Of Miguel

"Thank you, Mamá!" said Miguel. "A new box of crayons!"

Miguel had paper and pencils. He was ready!

It was the first day of school and Miguel couldn't wait. Today he would learn to read!

"Mama, what is for breakfast?" asked Miguel.

"Tortillas with scrambled eggs. A special breakfast for a special day," Mamá replied.

After breakfast, Mamá helped Miguel with his backpack and jacket. Then she dressed his baby sister, Sophia.

Together they left their little apartment on the third floor and walked to Miguel's school.

Along the way, Miguel looked at the writing on the store fronts and the billboards.

He looked up at the street signs.

Miguel knew the bus picture on the street sign was where his dad took the bus to work.

"I can't wait to read all these words by myself," thought Miguel.

His Mamá held his hand tight; and before Miguel knew it, they were at his school.

His Mamá gave him a hug. "Have a nice day, mi hiho!"

Miguel found his grade and his teacher, Mrs. Rodriquez, in the school yard.

As he walked into school Miguel waved "good bye" to Mamá and Sophia.

"Adiós!" Mamá called back.

Miguel knew the letters in his name: M-I-G-U-E-L. He was able to find his seat and he put his paper, pencils, and crayons in his desk.

Miguel saw the alphabet on the wall in the front of the room.

He saw books...so many books. He couldn't wait.

He was ready. Today he would learn to read.

Miguel had a great first day.

He liked his teacher. He made some new friends.

He learned where all the important places in the school were.

Miguel now could find the library, the nurse's office, the cafeteria, and the Principal's Office. From the big kids in his apartment, Miguel knew the Principal's Office was the one place no one wanted to go!

But after the day was over, Miguel still didn't know how to read.

Isn't that why he was going to school...to learn to read?

Mamá was waiting with Sophia in the school playground to meet Miguel after school.

"How was your day?" asked Mamá.

"Bueno! But I still don't know how to read."

"You will," said Mamá. "Little by little it will happen. You wait and see."

Miguel gave his mother the notes from Mrs. Rodriquez about class activities.

. . . .

When Miguel's dad came home from the restaurant that evening, Mamá had Papá read them.

"Miguel," said his father, "you need to bring in two dollars for a class trip to the zoo." His Papá gave him the two dollars and Miguel put the money in an envelope. He wrote his name on the envelope and put it right in his backpack. "Now, Miguel, choose a book. I will read you your bedtime story." said Papá.

In September Miguel learned all the alphabet names that were on the wall in front of the class.

In October and November, Miguel learned the sounds of the letters.

By December Miguel could put together some letters and sound them out to read.

The first word Miguel learned to read and spell was "cat". He had a cat, named Taco, who was as yellow as the corn tacos Mamá made. Miguel would go around the house spelling cat: c-a-t; and then trying to make some words rhyme with it: cat, fat, mat!!

Every night Miguel would practice his word cards with Papá as Mamá watched.

In January Mrs. Rodriquez gave the children a black-marbled notebook.

"This is your writing journal," said Mrs. Rodriquez.

"Every morning after you put your things away, you will write a sentence and draw a picture."

"You'll be an author!" proclaimed Mrs. Rodriquez.

Miguel couldn't wait!

So, on Monday morning when he got to school; Miguel got right to work. He took out his notebook and wrote as best as he could in his own spelling:

"Mamá took Sofa and me to the prk."

. . . .

Miguel took time to draw a picture of the swings and sliding board. Then he drew Mamá, Sophia, and himself.

Mrs. Rodriquez checked Miguel's book. "Please read me your sentence, Miguel."

Miguel read his words perfectly. "Great reading, Miguel," his teacher said.

Then Mrs. Rodriquez showed Miguel how to correctly spell, " Sophia" and "park."

That night Miguel took out his black -marbled notebook and read his journal to his Mamá, Papá, Sophia, and Taco.

"I can read!" Miguel said with a big grin.

Through February, March, and April, Miguel was writing more and more in his journal. Then every night, Miguel would read his stories to his family. Sometimes when reading to Mamá, Miguel saw Mamá following along with her finger under each word as he read.

One evening Miguel was reading a book that Mrs. Rodriguez sent home for the class to practice.

"Mamá, what is this word and this word?" Miguel asked.

"I don't know, mi hijo. Go next door to Mrs. Torres. She can help you, I'm sure," his Mamá replied.

At first Miguel didn't understand why Mamá would tell him to see Mrs. Torres. Why couldn't Mamá help him?

The more Miguel thought about this the more he thought about how Mamá never read to him before bed. Mamá never read the notes from school. She always had Papá read the mail. Then a little grin lit up his face. Miguel figured it out and he would help.

From then on, Miguel brought his black-marbled notebook home every night for Mamá.

First, they practiced the alphabet. Then they practiced the letter sounds and started to make words. Miguel used his flash cards and made some games for him and Mamá to play. The "Word Match Game" was his favorite. In the beginning, Miguel won most of the games; but little by little, Mamá started to win as well. Then one day, Miguel saw Mamá trying to read a note he brought home from school. Miguel watched but didn't say a word.

Mrs. Rodriquez noticed how Miguel would bring his notebook home every evening. She noticed how Miguel carried his notebook with him to the playground and to the bus. She wondered...

In May a special class project was assigned. The children had to write what they wanted to be when they grew up. All of the children were going to read their stories aloud in class.

Miguel knew exactly what he was going to write about. The story sharing began the following week. When it was Miguel's' turn, he got up and read his story perfectly to the class:

<u>The Teacher</u>

When I grow up, I want to be a teacher.

I want to teach my mom to read.

Then she can read to me.

She can read me my bedtime stories.

When I am big, I will teach kids to read.

They can come to my school.

Mrs. Rodriquez wiped a small, salty drop from across her cheek as she and the class clapped for Miguel.

JUNE
AUTHOR DAY
I have a son
TACO'S FUNNY ADVENTURES
The Teacher

In June the children could invite a special guest to school for "Author's Day". Miguel and his classmates would read and share a story they had written.

When the big day arrived, Miguel kept looking at the classroom clock. When would "Author's Day" begin? Finally, it was time. All of the guests were starting to come into the class.

"Hola! Mamá," said Miguel.

They sat together on the rug. Miguel read Mamá his story about his cat: <u>Taco's Funny</u> <u>Adventures.</u>

Both Mamá and Miguel laughed. "I love your story, Miguel!" said Mamá.

Then it was Mamá's turn. Miguel saw Mamá take out a paper.

Mama read:

"I have a son. His name is Miguel. He is seven years old.

He is a good boy. Because of my Miguel, I can read. I love him."

When Miguel squeezed Mamá's hand, his black -marbled notebook fell to the floor.

It flipped open to his story of "<u>The Teacher</u>".

Miguel smiled at Mamá. "I am a teacher!" he whispered. "I really am a teacher!"

"Yes, Miguel, you are!" Mamá whispered back. "You are!"

Glossary of Spanish words used with definitions and pronunciations:

1/ adiós (ah-dyohs) good-bye

2/ bueno (bweh-noh) good

3/ hola (oh-la) hello, hi

4/ Mamá (mah-mah) mother, mom

5/ Miguel (Mee-gehl) Michael

6/ mi hijo (mee ee-hoh) my son

7/ Papá (pah-pah) father, dad

8/ Sophia (So-fi-uh) Sophia, Sophie

9/ taco (tah-koh) a fried, corn flatbread, folded over with various fillings

10/ tortilla (tor-tee-uh) a thin round of corn or wheat flour bread with fillings or toppings

About the Author

Born in Brooklyn, New York and raised and educated in New Jersey, Julie Eller seemed to always find enjoyment in working with children. Their honesty, creativity, energy, and playfulness have always made her want to be part of their world. What better way to do that; but for her to become an educator. Julie Eller's undergraduate and Master's degrees in Education and Reading prepared her to spend her entire professional career teaching elementary school along with working with students at <u>The College of New Jersey.</u>

Julie Eller claims to have had a passion for reading and writing beginning at an early age which continues today. She has had stories and articles published in local magazines, newspapers, and educational journals. She shares that she is able to find a story in just about anything that is part of her life or in the world around her.

Julie's other interests include floral designing and gardening as part of being in a garden club. She also enjoys watercolor painting, golf, and spending time with her family; especially at the beach, where she resides and continues to find stories that need telling.

CPSIA information can be obtained
at www.ICGtesting.com
Printed in the USA
BVHW011343230223
659077BV00002B/39

9 781665 579698